D0966573

SASHA SAVVY LOVES TO CODE

by
SASHA ARIEL ALSTON

Illustrated by
VANESSA BRANTLEY-NEWTON

Publisher
Gold Fern Press
Washington, DC

Printed in the United States of America

Cover Design by Jana Rade

Sasha Savvy Loves to Code

ISBN 13: 978-0-9971354-2-8 (Hardcover)
ISBN: 978-0-9971354-3-5 (E-book)

First Printing: May 2017

Dedication

For Tracy Chiles McGhee, the best mom ever

CHAPTER 1

ONCE UPON A SUMMER BREAK

"Hey class! How about I read a book before summer break begins", Mr. Turner asks with a big grin.

"Yeah!" The class screams, with Sasha Savvy being the absolute loudest, sitting at the edge of her desk.

Sasha's rocking her brand new purple and sparkly "I'm Awesome" tee-shirt, which she saved especially for the last day of school. She listens closely to Mr. Turner read from one of her favorite stories, the one about the alien take-over in the land of Fashionboz.

The whole class thinks Mr. Turner with his shiny bald head and super cool white-rimmed glasses is the best teacher ever. He always makes reading fun by acting out the characters in different, funny voices and walking around the classroom instead of sitting still at his desk.

By the third chapter, though, Sasha loses focus and starts twirling her curly black hair looking between the clock and out of the window at the bright sunshine. Normally she pays attention but right now, she just wants to begin summer fun - going to camp, swimming at the community pool, having cookouts in her backyard and going to the mall with her cousins. Not only that, Sasha will visit her grandparents in California, have more sleepovers with her friends, and go on other adventures around Washington, DC. The Savvy's love to visit museums like the National Museum of African American History & Culture and the National Air and Space Museum. They also enjoy paddle boating on the Tidal Basin and going to music festivals. She looks back at the clock. In just a few minutes, fourth grade will be over and summer break will begin. 11:58...11:59....12:00pm! And the bell rings. With all eyes on Mr. Turner, he closes the book with a thump on the desk and says “That’s it, kids. Have a fun summer!”

“Yay!” Sasha yells, along with her classmates. She jumps out of her seat, heads to the front of the class, and gives Mr. Turner a high five. She then looks around and finds her friends Gabby and Ashley in the crowd and gives them big hugs and says good-bye. She will see them throughout the summer. Now, she needs to go meet her mom who is picking her up.

CHAPTER 2

DECISIONS, DECISIONS

Sasha races to her mom's silver jeep as fast as she can with her hair bouncing behind her. She hops in the jeep and says, "Hey mom! It's summer break!"

Her mom, Stacy Savvy, laughs and replies "That's right, Sasha. Now be safe and buckle up. Let's go to my office and have some lunch."

Sasha's mom is a software developer at a big technology firm. She knows all about how computers and technology works. She is smart, cool, stylish, and

Lizzie's Deli
Cafe
Specials

fun. She wears her hair short in a curly fro. They go on a lot of mommy/daughter adventures together and take lots of pictures. Sasha's grandmother calls them the Selfie Queens, which makes them laugh and take more pics. Every month, their favorite thing to do is going to the library and checking out a few books to read. Sasha loves to read and is a part of a cool book club with her best friends.

"We're going to your office? Yay."

Ms. Savvy drives by a lot of tall buildings. Sasha likes to count red, yellow, and green cars when riding because those are so rare. Finally they arrive on the street where Ms. Savvy works. She finds a perfect parking space in front of her own office building downtown on K Street, NW. In DC, there are four quadrants, or sections of the city. Many of the streets are named after letters of the alphabet and some of their cross streets are numbers. At times, it makes places easier to find.

"So Sasha, where do you want to go for lunch?

"Lizzie's! I want a turkey, cheese, lettuce and tomato sandwich with potato chips and a chocolate chip cookie."

"Love that you know exactly what you want but let's think of something else to get instead of those chips. We can go to the deli and bring lunch back to the office."

"Ok that's a great idea mom. I'm sooo hungry. My belly is growling."

Lizzie's Deli & Cafe is only two blocks away from Ms. Savvy's office. When they arrive, Dante and Ms. Savvy greet each other by their first names. She goes to this deli a lot for lunch and sometimes for dinner when she works late at the office. Dante already knows exactly what her favorite sandwich is and how she likes it. Sasha happily gives him her order. She gets an apple instead of chips. While they wait for the order to be completed, Ms. Savvy texts on her cell phone and Sasha plays a quick game on hers. Within a few minutes, their food is ready and they say their good-byes to Dante and also Miss Lizzie the owner, who bakes the best ooey gooey chocolate chip cookies in DC.

While walking back to the office, Sasha sees a homeless man sitting on the ground, holding a sign that says, "Help, I'm a Veteran."

"Mom, can I have some change so I can give it to the man?"

"Sure Sasha. That's Mr. George." Ms. Savvy has already given Mr. George money, a couple of sandwiches, a cup of coffee, and a lottery ticket within the last week. Sometimes, she stops to chat with him to and from the office. He has the best stories about growing up in Detroit and traveling the world when he was in the army. He also makes her laugh when it looks like she is having a bad day.

Sasha puts the money into Mr. George's hat.

He smiles and says "Thank you, little lady" and winks at Ms. Savvy.

They arrive back at the building and greet Marcus the Security Guard as they head towards the elevator. Ms. Savvy's office is on the 8th floor.

"So Sasha, check out my new office. "

"Oh, wow. I love it. You have a window now." She notices a picture of the two of them in a shiny silver frame on her mom's big deep chocolate brown L-shaped desk and smiles.

"Have you decided which class you would like to take for the summer camp's second session?"

"I don't know, mom. I'm already taking swimming lessons for the first session. Last year, I took tennis and the year before that I took golf lessons. I'm already good at those. I've tried ballet and played the piano after school. I even tried taking a drama class

but I didn't like any of those. I don't know what to do."
Sasha lets out a big sigh.

CHAPTER 3

BREAKING IT DOWN

Ms. Savvy looks at the camp options online.

"Ah! There's a new class called "Coding Rocks!" How about learning how to code?"

Sasha looks perplexed. "Code? What's that?"

"Well, this is what your mom does all day long and I love it."

"Mom, sorry but that doesn't sound like any fun. Besides I'm not that good with computer stuff."

"With computers, you can do so many things!

Coding is simply how you tell a computer how to do something or how to solve a problem in a language that it understands."

"Language? Talking to a computer? That sounds weird."

Sasha's mom gets up from her desk and writes C.O.D.E on the whiteboard in big letters with a special red marker. Then she turns to Sasha and says, "The C stands for Communicate. First, you get to choose the language for your coding project."

"Like Spanish," asks Sasha

"Kind of but I mean computer languages. There are several you can use. You simply choose the one best for your project," Ms. Savvy explains

"Oh," says Sasha.

"The O stands for Organize. The Computer understands best if you break things down in very simple step-by-step instructions like 1. 2. and 3."

"Hmmm... like Daddy's recipes when we cook together?"

"Yep! Exactly like that!

"OK I get to tell the computer what to do. This sounds easy so far."

"Great! Now, the D stands for Demonstrate. Once

the Computer understands the basic steps, you can ask it to show you what happens when it follows all of your instructions. This is what we call compiling and running the program."

"Wow, what does the "E" stand for?

"The E stands for Express. When the computer knows how to do exactly what you taught it without any errors, you can share what you've created or solved with others! Isn't that great?"

"That's fabulous!"

Sasha's mom grabs her cell phone and motions for Sasha to come closer to show her the screen. She shows her a game. "This game started with coding. Let me show you how."

"Wow" Sasha's eyes light up. So I can make my own game?"

"Yes! Not just that, you can design video games, create mobile apps, build robots, make digital movies, and other cool tech stuff. It all starts with coding."

"Omg, mom! This sounds sooo cool. I can't wait to go to camp so I can learn more about coding. I have to tell Gabby and Ashley all about this so we can go to the camp together."

"See. I told you it was fun. Soon you will love

coding just like I do."

"Like you? I don't know about that, mom. Don't get too excited."

Ms. Savvy giggles and gives Sasha a hug.

As Sasha and her mom get on the elevator to go downstairs to the daycare, Sasha repeats --- Communicate. Organize. Demonstrate. Express. --- Communicate. Organize. Demonstrate. Express.

CHAPTER 4

YOU ABSOLUTELY CAN

When Sasha and her mom arrive home, they go straight to the kitchen and find Sasha's dad, Steve Savvy chopping up onions. Mr. Savvy is wearing his favorite Howard University chef's apron over a checkered shirt. He graduated from there and Ms. Savvy graduated from Georgetown University. They met while they were in college.

"Dad! Savion! Guess what?"

Mr. Savvy looks up with a bright smile. Savion,

Sasha's older brother, is on his cellphone playing a basketball game app. He is fifteen and gives Sasha a quick nod while he keeps his eyes on the game. He almost has enough points to advance to the next level.

"Hey Sasha! Sorry I couldn't pick you up today but you know that Dad had a big catering event. How was your last day of school?" Mr. Savvy asks.

"It was great! And then Mom taught me how to code and it was amazing. I'm going to a coding camp in a month at the rec center."

"Wow, baby! You taught Sasha how to code already?"

Ms. Savvy laughs and gives him a kiss on the

cheek. "Yes, you can never learn too early."

"You're right. This is exciting. We're gonna have a little tech star!" says Mr. Savvy.

"Tech star? Now that's funny. Coding is a boy's thing." Savion insists while laughing.

"That's not true. I can do whatever I want to do." says Sasha, folding her arms and rolling her eyes at Savion.

Ms. Savvy laughs now. "That's right Sasha. You absolutely can. Savion, so what do you think your mama does all day at work? S.T.E.M. needs more girls!"

Savion just keeps playing his game.

"Wait, mom. What's S.T.E.M.?" Sasha asks.

"Sorry sweetie. That's just an acronym, a short way of referring to several words using the first letter of each word. S.T.E.M. stands for Science, Technology, Engineering and Mathematics. Remember, how I taught you an acronym for C.O.D.E, earlier?"

"Oh yeah. Gotcha!"

"Yes!" Savion scores, jumps up, and hugs his little sis. How about *that* you little Tech star?!"

Sasha smiles and breaks free from her brother. "Hey Dad, so what's for dinner?"

"I'm whipping up my famous turkey burgers and

sautéed spinach. How does that sound?"

Savion and Sasha ask in unison. "Sautéed spinach?!" What about fries?"

"Nope but I promise it will be the best spinach you have ever tasted. Now go wash your hands and get ready for dinner."

CHAPTER 5

SEEMS PRETTY COOL

Sasha's favorite day of the week is Saturday. She can sleep in and relax until Ms. Savvy is ready to run errands. They always run errands together. Mr. Savvy works on the weekends. He is a Chef for a new restaurant near the Navy Yard in SE Washington, DC.

When Sasha and her mom return from running errands and settle in, they hear the doorbell ring. Ms. Savvy goes to open it.

"Oh, Hi Perla. Hi girls! I totally forgot that you guys

were coming over today. It's been a busy week. Come on in," says Ms. Savvy.

"Hi Stacy. No worries. Glad the work week is over. Time to relax." says Ms. Reyes.

Sasha runs in and hugs Gabby and Ashley and they disappear into the family room to hang out.

Ms. Savvy and Ms. Reyes chat for a while in the kitchen before she leaves. Sasha, Gabby, and Ashley spread out on the floor and listen to their favorite songs while doing a craft project. They are creating bookmarks using markers, stamps, buttons, feathers, ribbon string, and glitter.

"Guess what I'll be doing next month!" Sasha asks.

"What!" Gabby and Ashley ask at the same time.

"I'm going to a coding camp at the rec center. We should all go together." says Sasha.

"Uh, what's coding?" says Gabby.

"It's the way you can talk to computers. My mom does it at her job." says Sasha.

"Computers? That sounds boring. I'm about to start tennis camp. I'm almost as good as Serena Williams." says Gabby.

Sasha laughs. "Yeah, you are pretty good at tennis. You can do tennis and coding if you want. Even though

I'm already good at it, I'm going to swimming camp again so I can get even better."

"I'm going to the dance camp this time, but I've heard of coding. My uncle is an engineer and I think he knows how to do that." says Ashley.

"That's cool Ashley. My mom says when you learn to code, you can make apps and games like the ones we use on our tablets." says Sasha.

"Wow! Really? I wanna make a game!" says Gabby.

"I know. Me too! You can do so many things with coding. I think we all should go." says Sasha.

"Count me in. So what do you think, Gabby?" asks Ashley.

"I'm down. It seems pretty cool."

"Ok, I'm gonna tell my mom so y'all can go too." says Sasha.

Sasha walks in the dining room while her mom is on her laptop working on a project for her job.

"Hey mom. I told Gabby and Ashley about the coding camp and they want to go too."

"That's awesome! I'll tell their parents about the camp tomorrow." says Ms. Savvy.

"Ok cool. This is gonna be the best summer ever!" Sasha proclaims as she skips off.

Ashley's mom, Ms. Webster, comes to pick up the girls the next day. Gabby lives on the way to their house so she can drop her off. Ms. Savvy gives Ms. Webster information on the coding camp so the girls can all go together. For the next month, Sasha, Gabby and Ashley go to museums, water parks and make ice cream sundaes with Ashley's grandmother when they aren't at camp.

CHAPTER 6

TODAY IS THE DAY

Today is the first day of coding camp and Sasha is so excited that she jumps out of bed and rushes straight to her parent's bedroom.

Knocking on the door, she yells, "Mom"! Dad!"

Ms. Savvy yawns and tells Sasha to come in. "What's wrong, baby?"

"Today is the day I learn how to be a coder. I can't wait to make my first app." says Sasha.

"Yes sweetie, that's great! But go get some more

rest. We have forty-five minutes before it's time to get ready." says Mr. Savvy.

Ms. Savvy laughs. "I'm so happy for you Sasha. But listen to your dad and go back to bed. I'll see you in a bit."

Sasha leaves her parents room reluctantly. When she climbs back into her comfy bed, she has the biggest smile on her face while she thinks about the cool things they will do at camp until she drifts off to sleep.

Ms. Savvy walks into Sasha's room painted in a bright sunshine yellow. "Ok Miss Tech Star, it's seven o'clock and time to get this day started.

Sasha opens her eyes, sits up, and stretches her arms. "OK I'm ready. Thanks mom. This is going to be the best day ever."

"Aww sweetie, you are so welcome. So glad that coding makes you excited. Now give me some sugah!" Ms. Savvy requested.

Sasha decides to wear her bubble gum pink romper and her favorite pink sneakers. She is officially ready to be a fashionista and coder. Sasha and Ms. Savvy head downstairs to have breakfast prepared by the Master Chef Steve Savvy.

“Good morning ladies! I present to you my veggie omelet made from a recipe in my very own cookbook. Bon appetit.” says Mr. Savvy.

“You are just too much dad!” says Sasha.

Mr. Savvy laughs, “Just try it. You won’t be disappointed.”

“Ooo la la. This is delish!” says Ms. Savvy.

“Yep. Totally yum,” says Sasha.

Mr. Savvy smiles, “I told y’all, but thanks. Enjoy your first day at coding camp. I love you both.” says Mr. Savvy.

“Love you too!” says Ms. Savvy and Sasha.

Ms. Savvy and Sasha drive twenty minutes to the rec center offering the coding camp.

“I will pick you up at 3:30 pm. You remember where to go, right?” says Ms. Savvy.

“Yes, mom, I got this.” says Sasha.

“Ok, well I love you and have lots of fun today” says Ms. Savvy.

Ms. Savvy kisses Sasha goodbye and watches Sasha until she sees her join Gabby and Ashley in front of the building.

CHAPTER 7

A ROUND OF APPLAUSE

"Hey Gabby and Ashley!" says Sasha.

"Hey Sasha!" they respond.

"What are y'all waiting for? Let's go in and get this coding party started!" says Sasha.

The girls are greeted by a woman wearing a red "Coding Rocks!" tee-shirt with white lettering.

"Hi young ladies! Are you here for the coding camp?" says Ms. Brown, the head counselor.

"Yes ma'am." says Sasha.

"Sounds great. So glad you're here. Just go to the lady with the other red tee-shirt so you can join the rest of the girls." says Ms. Brown.

"Ok, thanks!" says Ashley.

They walk into the room where the coding class is being held. Each table has a laptop, notebooks and pencils. There are so many girls and they are all different ages. They walk over to the table that has three unfilled seats. Once seated, the girls introduce themselves to the other girls and find out that they are thirteen. The camp counselor gathers the girls around to play a game so everyone can get to know each other. Sasha is the first one to start the game. She walks into the circle and says "My name is Sasha and I like to read!" Everyone says "Sasha likes to read!" and they all dance around and pretend they are reading books. After everyone says their name and favorite hobby, they are asked to go back to their seats.

"Ok girls, let's all have a seat so we can meet a few people. Next up is our three guest speakers. We have an App Developer, a Computer Programmer, and an Information Technology Program Manager."

Sasha enjoys hearing from people that love coding. Her interest is sparked. The lady in the blue dress created an app that her mom uses all the time to help her stay organized.

"Alright. Let's give these amazing ladies a round of applause. I hope everyone is ready for lunch. Today we're having pizza."

"Omg pizza. I love pizza. I can't wait!" says Gabby,

Sasha's table was the last to be called. She got two slices of cheese pizza while Gabby and Ashley got pepperoni. Her table played card games until lunch was over.

CHAPTER 8

LET'S TAKE A LOOK

"Ok young ladies. We're gonna start learning how to code now. Is everybody ready?!"

A room full of girls responds yes. The camp counselor hands out a glossary of keywords that they will need to know to code.

"Coding is a set of instructions a computer can understand based on many different languages, like HTML or Python. It explains exactly what you want it to do at any given time. For beginners, one of the best languages to learn is Java."

Sasha whispers under her breath, "Communicate".

"Everyone please open your laptops and go to the website listed on the sheet in the middle of the table. The first thing we will do is write out our name. String variables are created with adding String and placing the value in quotation marks. Type in String name, add an equal sign and place your name into the quotation marks. This creates a variable known as name and now your name is the value. Does everyone understand so far?"

A room full of girls nod their head yes.

Ms. Brown goes into further detail about the keywords and what's needed for a Java program. She writes everything on the whiteboard so they can see what's being described.

"Next, you will share your ideas using the System.out.print method. This method allows you to write cool sentences and statements. Type in System.out.print, and add parentheses around the variable name. After you are done, press the word Run below."

"Wow! It just printed my name!" says Gabby

"Mine too! This is awesome." says Sasha

All of the girls high five each other and go back to listening to the counselor.

"Unfortunately, sometimes, there may be mistakes, or bugs as we call them, in you code. When you have bugs, your code will not print. You have to always remember to add parentheses, quotation marks and semicolons for every sentence. Using the System.out. print method, we will write our birthday month, favorite singer and the color of our shoes. I will complete this project on the projector screen along with you so you can see how to set everything up."

"What does the semicolon do?" asks Ashley

"We have to end each statement with a semicolon. Please let me know if you have any questions. says Ms. Brown

Sasha says out loud what her mom taught her about coding steps, "Communicate. Organize. Demonstrate. Express.

"Sasha, what did you say? Is there something you want to share with the class?

"Well, my mom is a software developer and she shared a trick with me to remember the steps you do when coding."

"Wow, this sounds cool. Why don't you come to the front and share it with us."

Sasha explains all the steps and the class and Ms.

CODING
ROCKS

Brown clap for her. Then she gets so excited that she leads the class in a cheer.

"Give me a C!"

"C"!

"Give me an O!"

"O!"

Give me a D"!

"D"!

"Give me an E!"

"E"!

What's that spell?

CODE!

"Communicate. Organize. Demonstrate. Express!"

"Communicate. Organize. Demonstrate. Express!"

"Let'ssss go!"

Ms. Brown is excited and gives her a big thanks. Some of the girls give Sasha high fives as she returns to her seat.

"OK, settle down, everybody. I finished the project, so let's see if you can get your code to work."

Sasha types in all of the statements but nothing prints out. She gets errors. She looks at Ms. Brown's code and then back at hers over and over again and can't figure out why it isn't working. She gets really upset.

"Omg. This is too hard and I don't have any idea what's wrong." says Sasha.

One of the older girls at her table tries to help Sasha until Ms. Brown comes over.

"Hi Sasha, what seems to be the problem here?" she asks.

"I can't figure out why my project won't work. I hate coding!" says Sasha.

"Oh no! It's ok to make mistakes Sasha. Let's take a look at your code and see if we can find the bug. Did you include quotation marks everywhere you need them?"

Sasha looks carefully at her work. "Oops! I missed a quotation mark at the end of Pink. Thanks, Ms. Brown. I'm sure it will work this time! "

"You're very welcome. See if it works now."

Sasha excitedly runs the program again and gets an Error message *again*.

"What!? You've got to be kidding me. Everyone else's is working but mine."

"Hold on Sasha. Let me take another look." says Ms. Brown.

Ms. Brown looks through each line of code to see why the program isn't working.

“OK, I think I see where the problem is. Do you think you can figure it out?”

Sasha leans in and squints her eyes. “I see it! I forgot to add a semicolon after the quotation marks.”

"Yep, that’s it! Make sure that you always have a semicolon to end your statement. Ok, now try to run the program again.”

“OMG, everything prints out now! I can see my name, favorite singer, and the color pink. Thanks Ms. Brown.”

“Awesome! Just remember that with a lot of practice and hard work, you can figure out your own mistakes but never give up and ask for help when you need it.

“Ok, I will. Thanks!”

The class ends.

Sasha, Gabby and Ashley are all super proud. They just finished their first coding program. Their first day at camp is a success!

“I really like coding. What about y’all? asks Gabby.

“Yep! It’s fun trying to find the bug.” says Ashley.

“True. It was a little hard in the beginning but I’m glad I got through it. We gotta stick together with this. What do y’all think about making a gaming app we can all play?” says Sasha.

“Yes! It can be about fashion! “says Ashley.

“And reading books and swimming! says Sasha.

“And tennis too”, says Gabby.

“Ok great! Let’s do it. We can start a business”, Sasha adds.

They all skip to Ms. Savvy’s jeep wearing their new “Coding Rocks” tee-shirts.

Ms. Savvy is eager to know how their first day went.

“Well, how was it?”

“It was fantastic and guess what. I have a new name.”

“Really and what is that, my dear?”

“My name is Sasha “Tech” Savvy and I love to code!”

GLOSSARY LIST

COMMUNICATE:

Languages: Java, HTML, Python, and Ruby

ORGANIZE:

Object: a description of things

Method: statements that create an action

Variable: a value that you can change

Parenthesis: You use parenthesis at the beginning and ending of each sentence

Quotation marks: you use at the start of each sentence

Semicolon: a semicolon is used at the end of each statement before the parenthesis

DEMONSTRATE:

Compile: converts code to see if there are any errors

Run: shows the result of the code in a program

Bug: a mistake in the program

Debugging: fixing the mistake in a program

EXPRESS:

Sharing the finished result or product

CPSIA information can be obtained
at www.ICGtesting.com
Printed in the USA
BVHW042048230619
551346BV00013B/12/P

9 780997 135428